Hello, Dark

Written by
Wai Mei Wong

Illustrated by
Tamara Campeau

First published in Canada and the United States in 2021

Text copyright © 2021 Wai Mei Wong
Illustration copyright © 2021 Tamara Campeau
This edition copyright © 2021 Pajama Press Inc.
This is a first edition.

10 9 8 7 6 5 4 3 2 1

www.pajamapress.ca   info@pajamapress.ca

 Canada Council Conseil des arts
for the Arts   du Canada

 ONTARIO ARTS COUNCIL
CONSEIL DES ARTS DE L'ONTARIO
an Ontario government agency
un organisme du gouvernement de l'Ontario

Canadä

The publisher gratefully acknowledges the support of the Canada Council for the Arts and the Ontario Arts Council for its publishing program. We acknowledge the financial support of the Government of Canada through the Canada Book Fund (CBF) for our publishing activities.

Library and Archives Canada Cataloguing in Publication
Title: Hello, dark / by Wai Mei Wong ; illustrated by Tamara Campeau.
Names: Wong, Wai Mei, author. | Campeau, Tamara, illustrator.
Description: First edition.
Identifiers: Canadiana 20210156368 | ISBN 9781772782219 (hardcover)
Classification: LCC PS8645.O464 H45 2021 | DDC jC813/.6—dc23

Publisher Cataloging-in-Publication Data (U.S.)
Names: Wong, Wai Mei, author. | Campeau, Tamara, illustrator.
Title: Hello, Dark / by Wai Mei Wong ; illustrated by Tamara Campeau.
Description: Toronto, Ontario Canada : Pajama Press, 2021. | Summary: "A small child confronts his anxiety about the dark by befriending it. He thinks about the good things darkness provides—like safety for nocturnal creatures—then imagines the dark as a friendly companion made of shadow with whom he plays imaginary games, tells secrets, listens to music, and talks about beautiful things. The book concludes with an Author's Note about the Author's experience with sleep anxiety as an Early Childhood Educator"— Provided by publisher.
Identifiers: ISBN 978-1-77278-221-9 (hardcover)
Subjects: LCSH: Bedtime – Juvenile fiction. | Imaginary companions -- Juvenile fiction. | Fear of the dark – Juvenile fiction. | BISAC: JUVENILE FICTION / Bedtime & Dreams. | JUVENILE FICTION / Imagination & Play. | JUVENILE FICTION / Social Themes / Self-Esteem & Self-Reliance
Classification: LCC PZ7.W664He |DDC [E] – dc23

Original art created digitally
Cover and book design by Lorena González Guillén

Manufactured in China by WKT Company

Pajama Press Inc.
469 Richmond St. E Toronto, ON M5A 1R1

Distributed in Canada by UTP Distribution
5201 Dufferin Street Toronto, Ontario Canada, M3H 5T8

Distributed in the U.S. by Ingram Publisher Services
1 Ingram Blvd. La Vergne, TN 37086, USA

For Ethan, Nathan, and Hoi Chun
—W.M.W.

To Kyle. May your shadows help you grow
—T.C.

Hello, Dark.

People tell me you can't hear me,
but I know you do.

5

4

3

2

1

You creep in when the sun goes down.
You keep me wide awake and worrying:
what will you do once I'm asleep?

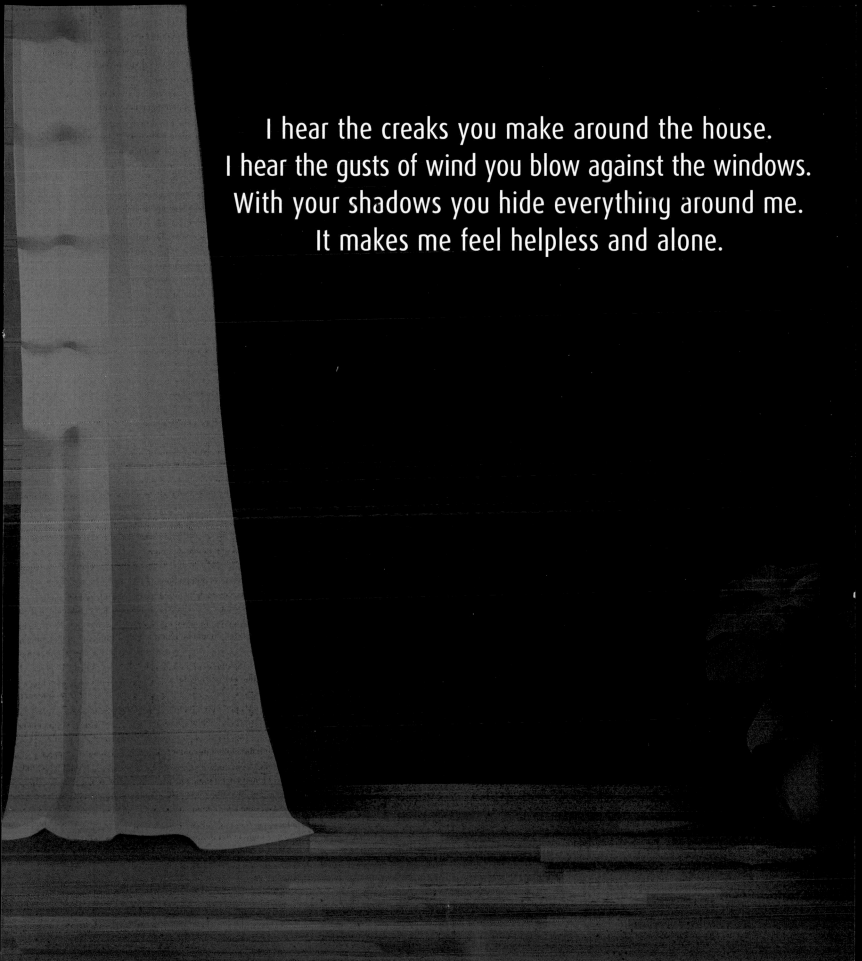

I hear the creaks you make around the house.
I hear the gusts of wind you blow against the windows.
With your shadows you hide everything around me.
It makes me feel helpless and alone.

I'm tired of being afraid of you.
Tonight, can we talk?

Are you always so scary?
You do some good things, too.

The starry sky and moon
shine brightly thanks to you.

I guess you're not so bad after all.
Maybe you don't want to be scary.
Maybe you're just lonely.

Hello, Dark.
Let's be friends.

We can talk about
happy things together.

We can play imaginary games
when nobody's watching.

We can count sheep.

We can practice breathing.

We can even listen to music until we fall asleep.

Tomorrow, if you meet me
at my night light,
I'm sure we can be friends.

Good night, Dark, my friend.

AUTHOR'S NOTE

As an Early Childhood Educator, I frequently encounter families who are seeking support to manage their children's fear of the dark. *Hello, Dark* was inspired by this concern and the strategies I have shared with families.

While young children's imaginative minds develop, it is common for them to have nighttime fears. *Hello, Dark* acknowledges that children's experiences are very real to them. It encourages children to express their insecurities so they can take charge of their worries. The story suggests reframing the dark in a positive context, such as how darkness helps night animals thrive, and helps the stars and moon shine. *Hello, Dark* also mentions some techniques that may help ease sleep anxiety, like mindful breathing, thinking happy thoughts, listening to music, or offering security objects.

I hope you enjoy *Hello, Dark*. Providing children and families with support for emotional learning is a passion that is close to my heart.

—Wai Mei Wong